First published in the United States 1993
by Dial Books for Young Readers
A Division of Penguin Books USA Inc.
375 Hudson Street
New York, New York 10014

Published in Great Britain
by HarperCollins Publishers Ltd
Text copyright © 1993 by Jenny Nimmo
Pictures copyright © 1993 by Angela Barrett
All rights reserved
Printed in Great Britain
First Edition
1 3 5 7 9 10 8 6 4 2

Library of Congress Cataloging in Publication Data
Nimmo, Jenny.
The witches and the singing mice / Jenny Nimmo ;
pictures by Angela Barrett.
p. cm.
Summary: A retelling of a Celtic tale in which two cats
set out to save children in a Highlands village who have been
put under a sleeping spell by three wicked witches.
ISBN 0-8037-1509-9
[1. Folklore—Scotland.] I. Barrett, Angela, ill. II. Title.
PZ8.1.N58Wi 1993 398.21—dc20 [E] 92-37642 CIP AC

The WITCHES
ᢒ and the ᢒ
SINGING MICE

retold by Jenny Nimmo

pictures by Angela Barrett

Dial Books for Young Readers  *New York*

On a stormy night, when wolves still roamed the Highlands, three witches came to Glenmagraw. No one saw them come but Tam, the blacksmith's cat, and Rory, the carpenter's cat, who were watching from the barn.

Through the scream of the wind and the rumble of thunder, the cats' sharp ears picked up the sound of hoofbeats. A horse was toiling up the road, and a heavy wagon creaked behind it.

The cats crouched low in the hay, wondering what kind of human could be traveling on such a night, and when the wagon passed, they shuddered from the tips of their whiskers right through to the tufts at the ends of their thick furry tails.

Three dark figures were leaning into the wild wind; one held a whip, one held a lantern, and the third stared into the barn with terrible glittering eyes.

I smell mischief," hissed Tam.

"I smell worse, Brother," grunted Rory. "We must rest well, for I believe it might be the last good sleep we'll get for many a night."

But the cats slept fitfully. Strange sounds disturbed their dreams, a clattering and a hammering that had nothing to do with the weather.

By the next morning the storm had rolled away. The sun burst over the hill, and the villagers of Glenmagraw bustled into the street. There they scratched their heads and murmured in disbelief, for overnight the tumbledown building on the hill had been given a new roof; the crooked walls had been patched with stones; and smoke poured from the chimney.

"Who can be living there?" asked Andrew MacBride, the blacksmith.

"And who would build a house with only a peephole for a window?" asked Kirsty, his daughter.

"Who could work on such a stormy night?" asked Alec Ross, the carpenter.

"A magician?" suggested his son, Jamie.

"Or a witch?" said Kirsty.

"What nonsense you children talk," laughed the blacksmith and the carpenter.

But Kirsty and Jamie walked away from the laughter and headed up the hill, eager to see who could be living in the windowless house. They had not climbed far, however, when someone emerged from the house on the hill. The figure wore a hooded gray cloak that hung over her face in heavy folds, and she moved toward the children like a dark pillar of smoke.

Kirsty and Jamie ran helter-skelter down the hill, wanting only to be safe from that cloudy figure.

"Slow down, Child," said Kirsty's father as she raced into the yard. "Have you seen a ghost?"

"Not a ghost, Father, a . . . a . . ." but she could not finish, for there, moving soundlessly into the yard, was the stranger in her gray shroud.

"Good day, and what can I do for you?" asked Andrew MacBride, a little shaken by his mysterious visitor but determined to be polite.

"Blacksmith, I want you to make me a bed," she said, and her voice sent a chill through the man. "A big iron bed," she said, "with a bronze moon at the head and a bronze star at the foot. And I want it tonight."

"I cannot make you a bed by tonight," said Andrew MacBride, standing his ground. "I have work to do for other folk. Come back in three days and I'll see what I can do."

"You will do what I want, today!" she screeched.

"Woman, I will not," said the blacksmith firmly.

Then it will be the worse for you," snarled the woman, and as she whirled away, she turned on Kirsty such a furious glance that Kirsty, feeling dizzy, knelt and clung to her big cat, Tam.

"Stay with me tonight, Tam," she begged, "for I dread to be alone in the dark while that strange woman roams around."

And Tam murmured softly against Kirsty's cheek.

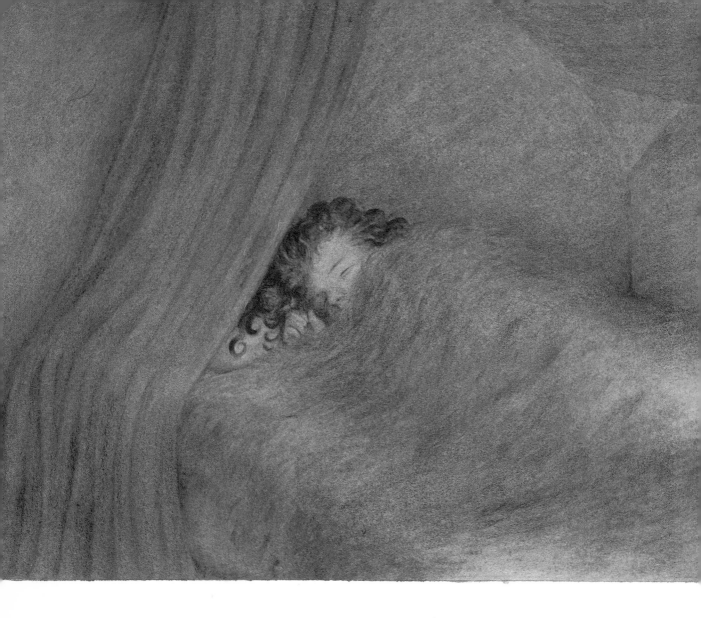

That night the big tomcat followed Kirsty when she went to bed. He curled himself comfortably at her feet, and heard her drift into her dreams. But Tam steeled himself for a sleepless and watchful night.

He saw the moon sail into the sky. He smelled the dew on the grass and he closed one eye. It would be so good to have a little nap, but he knew he must not.

He listened for footfalls, for anything that might bring harm to little Kirsty, but all he heard were owls crying and bats calling and faraway a drowsy, dreamy song. It was such delightful music that only the fairies could have made it. He yawned and closed his other eye. Surely Kirsty would come to no harm if he slept for just a minute or two.

Tam woke up feeling an unnatural chill in the room. Kirsty was lying cold and still, too still. He gently patted her cheek, but she did not stir. Tam felt the chill strike deep inside him.

"Kirsty!" called Mrs. MacBride. "Get up, Lassie. Come and help me in the kitchen."

Kirsty did not move.

Tam raised his head and such a dreadful wail tore out of him, Mrs. MacBride came running into the room.

"Whatever is it, Tam?" she cried, and then she saw Kirsty's face, deathly pale on the patched pillow. She shook her daughter and called her name over and over, but Kirsty was held fast in some terrible enchantment. And as her mother desperately rubbed the slender fingers, Tam saw four tiny toothmarks on Kirsty's wrist, and he was filled with shame. Mrs. MacBride saw them too.

"You wretched cat," she cried. "A mouse has bitten our Kirsty and poisoned her, and all the while you slept beside her. Shame on you for being a lazy good-for-nothing."

Tam did not wait to hear any more. He ran out of the house and crept under a thornbush. And there he stayed, disgraced, watching Kirsty's window.

He saw Granny Pine, the oldest and wisest in all the village, as she arrived at the house. She had brought her magic stick and her basket of herbs, and as Andrew MacBride drew her inside, there was a gleam of hope in his eyes. But when they came out, the hope was gone.

"It's the singing mice," she said, and shook her head. "One bite and the victim sleeps forever."

"That cannot be," argued the blacksmith. "The singing mice disappeared in my father's time, and they've never been heard of since."

"Well, they're back," said Granny Pine. "There's no doubt of it. And I cannot undo their sorcery." She looked sadly at her willow stick and her basket of herbs. "But there is a chance," she murmured thoughtfully, and she whispered something into the blacksmith's ear that seemed to cheer the man.

"Tam!" the blacksmith called.

But Tam would not go to him. He would not go to the house for his evening meal. He would not join Rory who called to him from the rooftops. He lay all night beneath the thornbush, watching Kirsty's window. And in the morning he stayed there still, cold and hungry as he was.

Rory did not understand why his friend crouched alone all day and would not talk to him. Puzzled and lonely, he went to play with Jamie in the carpenter's yard. He was chasing a cotton reel under the cart when he felt an icy wind blast into the yard, and the fur on the back of his neck bristled uncomfortably.

There in the gateway stood a motionless figure. She was wrapped in a black fleece and was taller than her sister, and fiercer.

"It's a fine day," said the carpenter, trying to be pleasant. "Can I help you?"

I want a cupboard," the woman demanded, "a big, oak cupboard with ivy leaves carved on the door, and I want it tonight."

"You're teasing, woman," the carpenter replied. "I have no oak cupboards and I certainly can't make one in a day."

"Then it'll be the worse for you," said the woman, and as she turned away, her green witch's eyes rested on young Jamie, who was chasing Rory and did not see the look.

That night Rory paced the rooftops calling for Tam to join him. His bright eyes searched the fields for a sign of movement, but it was a bitter, frosty night and no rats or voles were stirring. Then he heard the soft crunch of a footfall on the icy ground, and saw a small figure drift across the street, as in a dream. Young Jamie was making for the dark house on the hill. Swift as a hawk, Rory leapt off the roof and was after the boy, but on the hill path a sound of wonderful soft singing surrounded him. It filled him with longing, and he knew why the boy was drawn to it. He sank into the bracken, not knowing if he was tumbling into the song or the song into him, and at last he fell into a sweet, dreamless sleep.

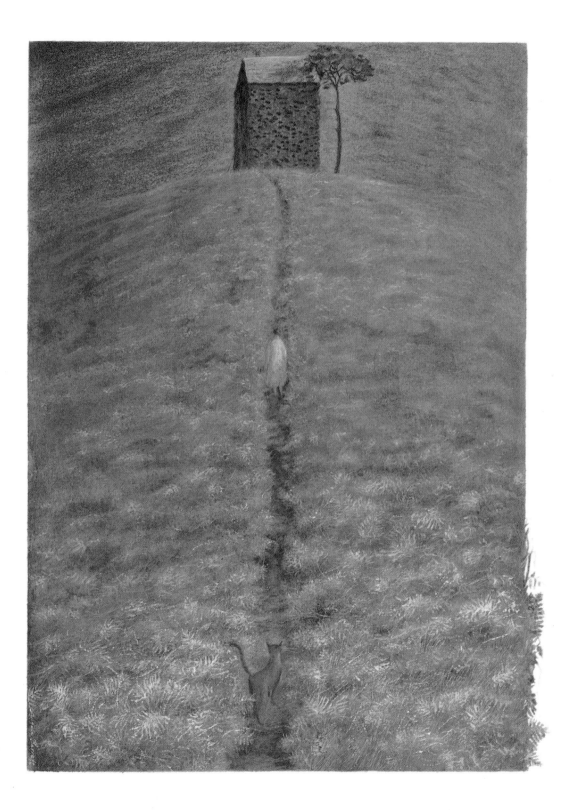

The next morning Alec Ross found his son fast asleep on the doorstep. He was stiff and cold in his nightshirt, and his father could not wake him. As he carried Jamie into the house, the carpenter saw four tiny toothmarks on the boy's wrist and he knew that his son suffered from the same dreadful sickness as Kirsty MacBride.

"What use is a cat," cried Mrs. Ross, flying at Rory with a broom, "if he can't keep a mouse from our door?"

"There's more than mice at work here," said the carpenter. "Why should our son leave his bed on a frosty night? Sorcery, that's what it is!"

Rory slunk away, ashamed and sad. He met Tam in the street, and the two cats strolled together, sharing their terrible news. As they passed the weaver's cottage, they felt a hush behind them, like an indrawn breath that swallowed even bird-song.

The two cats ducked into the shadow of a plum tree close by the weaver's door. They saw a woman cloaked in dark feathers and smelling of bones and mildew, taller than her sisters and even fiercer. She rapped on the door and when the weaver opened it, she said in a cruel voice, "Weaver, I want a hundred yards of black cloth, and I want it tonight!"

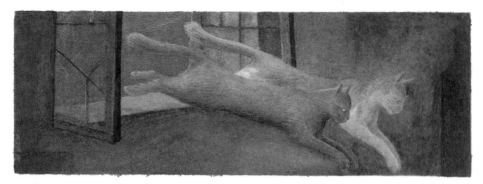

A hundred yards?" exclaimed the weaver. "I have no black cloth, and I cannot weave it all in one day. Such a task is impossible."

"Then it'll be the worse for you!" said the woman, and as she whirled away, her deep eyes darted past the weaver to the baby girl who slept in his wife's arms.

The dark figure swooped up the hill in her gloomy crow colors, and the two tomcats gazed helplessly at each other.

"We must do something," said Rory, "or like Kirsty and Jamie, that poor baby will sleep forever."

"Let us go to Granny Pine," suggested Tam. "Her herbs may be useless against the sleeping sickness, but she is still the wisest in the village. She will surely give us some advice."

Granny Pine was out on the hill, so the cats jumped through her window. They gazed at the herbs and the berries and heather; so many bright bottles, so many fragrant bowls. They crept close to her fire to wait.

Well, it's Tam and Rory, is it?" said Granny Pine, and twilight followed her into the room. "Come for advice, have you?"

The cats rubbed their heads in the soft folds of her skirt, and looked up at her.

"There is a way to cure Kirsty and Jamie," said the old woman. "If you can bring two freshly killed singing mice to the blacksmith and the carpenter, their children will be saved. But you must stay awake through the bewitching song, or you are lost!"

The cats sat back and listened anxiously.

"Those mice are not bad creatures," Granny Pine told them, "but wicked strangers have frightened them, and now they're singing for their very lives."

Tam and Rory growled low in their throats.

"Watch those witches and follow them," said Granny Pine. She tapped each cat with her willow wand, and for a moment they glimmered like fairy creatures. "A little magic to give you strength," she said. "Be off with you now, for soon those witches will be on the move."

Tam and Rory walked out into the starlight. Their tails were high and their golden eyes beamed eagerly into the night.

A thin pine yawned over the witches' wrinkled roof, and when the cats reached the house, they skimmed up to a branch beside the peephole window.

Peering into the room, they saw a round table with a tall candle in the center. The flames guttered in a draft that blew down the chimney, and strange shadows danced across the walls. Now the cats could see the witches; their hoods were down and their long hair straggled on their bony shoulders. Their faces were gray, their eyes were green, and they wore dreadful glinting, sharp-toothed smiles. The witches reeled around the room, and as they did so, their features began to change and the dark flying shapes were pierced with glittering eyes, flashing teeth, and knife-edged silver claws.

All at once and with a deafening shriek the dancing ended. The witches seemed to have vanished, and in their place three huge black cats paced around the room. They polished their whiskers and sharpened their claws, then snapping at shadows, they ran out of the door.

"We must follow!" Tam whispered.

"At a distance," said Rory. "If they see us, we will never solve this mystery."

Silent and skillful, Tam and Rory climbed out of the tree. The three black cats were heading toward the forest on the other side of the hill. Even the men from Glenmagraw seldom hunted there, for it was wolves' territory and a dark and dangerous place. But the two tomcats, thinking only of Kirsty and Jamie, moved soundlessly after the witches.

As they drew near to the forest, sweet music issued from the trees and the two cats began to falter. They sat back on their haunches, their heads spinning, and looked at each other in dismay.

The singing mice," breathed Rory. "We are lost, Brother. I am falling asleep."

Frosty moonlight spilled onto the hill, and the cobwebs that festooned the bracken glittered like strands of diamonds. Tam glanced drowsily at Rory, and sweeping at the cobwebs, he thrust a pawful deep into each ear. Without a word Rory did the same. Deaf now to the bewitching song, they sped down the hill, anxious not to lose sight of the witches. When they reached the trees, however, the three black cats had vanished.

Trusting in their sixth sense, Tam and Rory entered the forest. Ancient trees grinned and threatened, tangled roots caught and tripped the nimble paws, but the proud tomcats pressed on until they found themselves on the fringe of a glade lit by flames. The three black cats were circling a fire, and their smiles were so wild and wicked that Tam and Rory almost turned back at the sight of them. But as their eyes became accustomed to the fierce light, they saw small gray shapes moving beneath the trees, and they knew they had found the singing mice.

Tam and Rory leapt into a tree just as the black cats ceased their wild walk. They faced the crowd of little gray mice, and one of the cats stepped forward.

The mice stared up at her fearfully, and Tam and Rory swept the cobwebs out of their ears. The glade was silent; a witch was about to speak.

"Mice," she said, "you have pleased us. You have punished the blacksmith and the carpenter, but it is not enough. Today the weaver refused me. He has a baby. You must sing it to sleep and bite it. If you do not, you know what will happen!" And she raised a paw that glittered with razor-sharp claws.

Out from the crowd crept two mice; a streak of silver ran down each gray back, and between their ears they wore tufts of white fur like tiny crowns.

W e have decided not to harm any more children," said the first mouse.

"You will do as we say, King-mouse," snarled the cats, "or we will kill every one of you."

"We have made our decision," piped up the second mouse. "We will not bite children!"

"Foolish Queen-mouse!" shrieked the witches, and they pounced upon the little mice and struck them with their terrible claws.

The two royal mice rolled over and lay still.

"We must finish those witches, once and for all," whispered Tam, and together he and Rory leapt from their tree onto the three black cats.

The witch-cats had claws that burned, they had teeth that sank into the very bone and the strength of a hundred cats. But Tam and Rory clung on until even their eyes began to fail. They thought they must be fighting in their sleep and that when they woke, they would find themselves in the barn.

But when Tam and Rory opened their eyes at last, they were in the forest and the taste of blood told them they had not been dreaming. Beside them were three motionless forms.

Dead!" said Rory. "And look, there are the king and queen of the singing mice."

With but one thought the two cats each picked up a tiny body, and holding them gently in their mouths, they crept out of the glade.

The villagers were awake. Sounds from the forest had invaded their dreams, and they were gathered in the street, bewildered and afraid.

"Look there!" said Alec Ross as two shadows limped over the brow of the hill.

When the two tomcats hobbled into the lamplight, they were so bedraggled, they could scarcely be recognized. But Andrew MacBride exclaimed, "Why, it's Tam and Rory. You brave tomcats! You have brought us singing mice."

The blacksmith and the carpenter took the two little mice and placed them under their children's pillows, while Granny Pine gathered the cats into her arms. But even after she had rubbed ointment into their wounds, they would not rest.

"We must keep watch," they said, and they went to sit, each on his own roof under the stars. They did not move until they heard the cries of joy in the houses beneath them as Kirsty and Jamie woke up.

"They are safe!" sighed Tam.

What a fuss the children made of their two wounded heroes. There was so much cuddling and kissing, stroking and tickling, Tam and Rory purred themselves hoarse.

"It's a strange thing," the blacksmith remarked, "but the mouse we put under Kirsty's pillow had disappeared by this morning."

"So had ours," replied the carpenter.

Tam and Rory looked toward the hill and thought of the dark forest beyond. The singing mice would be welcoming their king and queen. For surely in dying for a child those two good mice had regained their lives.

The three witches were never seen again, and whenever the people of Glenmagraw mentioned them, a little anxiously, at dusk or at the onset of a storm, Granny Pine would say, "You're quite safe, you know, with Tam and Rory here."

And Tam and Rory would prick up their proud torn ears and lift their battle-scarred tails, and parade together down the street. And no one who saw them ever doubted that they were the bravest tomcats in all the Highlands.